MW00880353

Illustrations: Chantal Seddon

First published in 2019 by Restawhile Publishing

A CIP catalogue record for this book is available from the British Library.
ISBN: 978-1-9160303-0-5

RESTAWHILE PUBLISHING

www.restawhilepublishing.com
restawhilepublishing@gmail.com

Author: Phyllis Clifford
Illustrator: Chantal Seddon
Cover and Interior Layout: Pickawoowoo, Author Services

Printed & Channel Distribution:
Lightning Source | Ingram (USA/UK/EUROPE/AUS)

DEDICATION

Inspired by John Samways

CHAPTER ONE

"Bye dad," shouted Jamie and Lulu in unison still trying to put the lead on Missy's collar as they were heading out the front door.

"OK, bye," said their Dad, Jim, while holding his hand over the mouthpiece of the phone. "Don't forget the envelope for Mr Muckle," he reminded them.

"Yes," replied the twins.

Missy was used to the 6pm routine walk along the lane and around the corner to collect Solar.

"Hi Mr Muckle," they both said whilst looking over the hedge into his garden. But all they could see was his bottom in the air as he was on his hands and knees looking around his lawn.

"Found any yet?" they both enquired giggling.

"Ahh, yes and enough for the next few days," he said as he slowly stood up brushing off his trouser legs. "Carry on, he's inside and his lead is hanging in its usual place," he added smiling.

Solar woke up and wagged his tail when he saw the trio coming towards the back door. He stretched, yawned and was ready for his evening exercise.

"Hi Solar," said Jamie and Lulu as they stroked him, gesturing with their hands that it was time. Missy licked Solar's ears, and as the twins turned to go back out the door they placed the envelope from their Dad on Mr Muckle's kitchen table.

As all four left the long grey haired, jolly man said, "Don't forget tonight is the meteor shower around 11pm onwards and I will have my observatory roof open as I need to use my big telescope for this one," he exclaimed excitedly.

"OK, we'll let Dad know as well," smiled Jamie and Lulu.

'Hey Mr Muckle, is there really a man on the moon?' asked Jamie chuckling as they started to walk off up the lane.

'I would like to think so,' he shouted after them with a grin on his face. 'Maybe one day I might just find out', he thought as he smiled to himself and turned, shut the door and hobbled slowly through the gap in the hedge to his dear old friend's house next door, Molly. Mr Muckle and Miss Molly O'Shea ate together every evening at 6.30pm.

CHAPTER TWO

Jim put the phone down and punched the air and gave a big, "Woo-hoo, yes!"

"Hey you two....," Dad called.

"We know, we're on our way," Jamie said trying to slow Missy down as she made for the door.

"...another insurance deal sealed and it's the fifth this week," Jim shouted to the children who were half way down the garden path. "Please let our dear friend, and my old work mentor, know that I'm pulling the deals in left right and centre, won't you?"

Jim continued until the two were out of sight, as he closed the front door.

Five minutes later.

'Hi Mr Muckle, did you see anything in the sky last night?' asked Lulu.

'Are the meteor showers bright, sparkling and colourful as well?' enquired Jamie

'One of the best, you two, one of the best last night,' he said grinning as he bent down to feed dandelions to Tommy the tortoise and inform him about the upcoming Moon phenomenon. 'It just gets better and better with each viewing.'

Tommy just munched the flowers.

'Carry on you two and do let your Dad know that there is a Super Moon at the end of this month — and the roof will be open to see the spectacular view,' smiled the old man.

'We will let him know but he's always busy selling insurance and told us to let you know he has made five deals the week,' said Lulu with a sigh.

'Your Dad was always competitive even when we both worked together, but I gave all that up ten years ago when I dedicated my time to what I love best — the Moon,' announced Mr Muckle with a broad grin on his face to his two little friends.'

'We'll see who's right,' he said to himself. This Super Moon will show me more of its secrets which I've been dreaming of for the past nine years.

"Hey Mr Muckle, Dad said don't forget the insurance for your mobility scooter this week as well," Jamie informed him as he was trying to disentangle Missy's and Solar's leads from his legs.

"Your Dad never misses a trick when it comes to his insurance business, anything that isn't 'outer space' your Dad's onto it," he chuckled quietly to himself.

CHAPTER THREE

"Here we are Mr Muckle, here are some lettuce leaves from our garden for Tommy," said the twins as they gave the tasty treat to him for Tommy's dinner.

"Oh thank you, but before you go..." he beamed as he hobbled back inside his house,

"...this is for your Dad." He gave the twins an envelope. Missy and Solar both had their leads in their respective mouths and were now sitting watching and waiting.

Jamie and Lulu looked at each other, hesitated, and asked, "Is this the insurance for Tommy?" They both broke out laughing loudly taking the envelope.

"Hey you two, Tommy indeed...ah yes," said Mr Muckle now wide-eyed. He paused and said, "Let's make one up for him now!"

Mr Muckle fetched a piece of paper and wrote:

Saturday 20th June 2018
I, Mr Morgan Muckle,
Bequeath Tommy Tortoise,
his house and grounds
plus Solar
of
Star Gaze Cottage,
Scratchy Bottom Lane,
Puddlemix
Dorset
to
Jamie and Lulu Coverit,
if anything should happen to me.
Signed: Morgan Muckle
Witnessed................

"OK you two, sign your names and I'll ask Miss Molly from next door to witness it as well, that'll make your Dad laugh," he giggled as he handed the piece of paper to the pair to sign.

The aforementioned form was dated and signed by all including Molly, so when the twins came back from their walk with Solar, he gave them an envelope:

Jim Coverit

Only to be opened in an emergency

"This is so funny, Dad will love the joke," laughed Jamie as they both headed home with Missy.

CHAPTER FOUR

"Hi Mr Muckle," greeted the dripping wet twins in their wet weather gear as they stood at his back door.

Missy pushed past the humans in the doorway and left wet paw prints on the kitchen floor as she made her way over to greet and lick Solar's face.

"I'm off for the next week, so I'll leave the key in the usual place. Please look after Solar and Tommy for me until I get back, you know where everything is," their old friend asked the twins. Not an unusual request from him, but unusual in that it's for more than two days.

"OK Mr Muckle," said Jamie as he put his hood back up again.

"Oh, and tell your Dad as well that I've done it," he added.

"We will," they replied not sure what he meant but hoping their Dad would understand.

The rain was falling so hard it was bouncing up off the path as all four of them headed quickly on their soggy walk up the lane.

CHAPTER FIVE

As 6pm ticked over the twins were just heading off on their evening routine when there was a knock at the door.

The twins opened the door and shouted back into the house to their Dad. 'Dad, it's a policeman and another man at the door.'

Jim came to the door, phone to his ear, and gestured to the official looking men to come in and pointed for them to go through to the lounge. Everyone followed.

They all stood still and just looked at each other.

In that moment the smaller man spoke. 'My name is Mr Overwrite, an insurance inspector, and this is Constable Gottem from the local Piddlemix police station,' he announced formally to the assembled family.

'Yes, yes,' said Jim still talking into his phone.

'We are here to inform you that Mr Muckle is missing,' Mr Overwrite continued. 'We think Mr Muckle was one of the passengers on the one-way Moon flight MI Luna-tic that was launched on Saturday 1st September 2018 at 1pm.'

'Ahem,' interrupted Constable Gottem clearing his throat. 'Sorry, sir it was 3pm,' the constable said correcting Mr Overwrite.

'3pm,' the insurance inspector repeated and continued, giving a sideways glance at the Constable, '3pm...from Cape Canaveral, Brevard County, Florida, USA.' The insurance inspector said as he concluded his formal address.

Jim, slowly took his phone away from his ear, put it on silent and placed it in his lap. Jamie, Lulu and Missy just sat down and listened.

Mr Overwrite took a second breath and continued to the now opened-mouthed collective sitting quietly in front of the officials. Missy gave a sigh and held her head quizzically to one side.

"This is an insurance matter which is why we have come to your house Mr Coverit," he said to the now puzzled Coverit family.

"Ahh, is it about the mobility scooter?" Jim asked the inspector hesitantly.

"Err, not exactly Mr Coverit," replied Mr Overwrite to Jim's question.

"The sailing dinghy?" Jim queried further.

"No, sir, in fact it's Master and Miss Coverit we are here to speak to," Constable Gottem explained then turned to face the minors and cleared his throat.

"Master Jamie and Miss Lulu Coverit. We are here to inform you that owing to Mr Muckle now missing presumed...err, well not coming back..." stumbled Constable Gottem, "the authorities represented here by Mr Overwrite from the insurance company, and myself, Constable Gottem, have to inform you that you are joint beneficiaries of Mr Muckle's estate, chattels and goods therein."

Constable Gottem continued.

"The List includes:"

1. House.
2. All the goods inside and outside the house.
3. Solar and Tommy.
4. 'Colossal' Amateur Telescope, 1.8 metre (70-inch), rainbow coloured, with a diary of future celestial events.
5. Mobility scooter.

The stunned, silence was broken by...

Jamie who jumped up and said, "Dad, it's 6.05pm and Solar will be waiting for us."

Jim thanked Mr Overwrite the insurance inspector and Constable Gottem and acknowledged they would continue this conversation soon before escorting them to the front door.

Just before they left to collect Solar and Tommy, the twins produced the envelope that Mr Muckle had given to them.

'Dad, sorry I forgot about this letter and it might help explain why we had the visit tonight from the officials,' said Lulu looking slightly guilty that she had forgotten to give it to him weeks ago.

Jim, Jamie, Lulu and Missy left as well and walked around to Mr Muckle's house and greeted Solar who was waiting patiently by the back door for her daily visitors.

Jim went straight in to the Observatory, opened the roof and pointed the 'Colossal' Amateur Telescope towards the Moon. The twins followed with the curious Missy and Solar in tow. Jim zoomed the powerful Telescope up and in and towards the Moon.

"Wow," exclaimed Jim. "I should never have doubted my old friend, he just loved watching the Moon, and with his amazing telescope, and more than anything that was his dream – not selling insurance," Jim said shaking his head in disbelief.

And there it was...

A rocket. A rocket on the Moon and with two faces at the port hole waving. Mr Muckle and Miss Molly! "Wow, he was right, it is a great telescope and I really didn't believe him that he would do it and make his dream come true," said Jim.

Jim, Jamie and Lulu, with smiles on their faces tears in their eyes, all waved back even though their dear old friend couldn't see them.

"Mr Muckle was right, there is a man in the Moon," exclaimed Jamie and Lulu.

THE END

CPSIA information can be obtained
at www.ICGtesting.com
Printed in the USA
LVHW071612190919
631553LV00024B/129/P